The
Mustache Fairy

To every kid who wishes for the magic of facial hair. — *AAD*

My grandma's house is older,
And it's usually not scary,
But catching fireflies last month,
I came up with a fairy!

I had him caught in my two
hands,
And slowly peeked inside...

Wings! Glowing eyes! A furry face!
He had no place to hide.

He said, "Okay, you caught me,
Go ahead and make your wish."

I knew right off I wanted a pet. "How 'bout a talking fish?"

He looked uncomfortable and grumped,
"I don't know if you care, but the only kind of
wish I grant has to do with facial hair."

I took him to the bathroom and
looked hard at my face.
I'd never thought about it much,
but there is a lot of space.

I took my time and thought and
thought, 'til my fairy had the goes.

Then I wished for a long, full beard,
so I wouldn't need my clothes.

At breakfast, Grandma was surprised.
She really had a fright,

**To see the long, unruly beard
I'd grown just overnight.**

She looked me up, she looked me down.
She carefully inspected,

And wasn't very happy when she found that I was nekked.

She told me we would need to learn exactly how to shave,
'Cause I'm the only kid my age with a beard that won't behave.

So she took me to the barber, who used
some shaving cream,
Clippers and a razor, and a washcloth with
some steam.

And Grandma, she was happy. She whistled home. And then,

Looked at me to find—my beard was back again!

Grandma kept on trying, but I was
glad to have my fuzz.

I grew it long, scratched a lot, and fluffed it. Just because.

But finally summer ended and I
knew I had to fix

Being the only kid in class who had
a beard at six.

But I was fearsome tired of being called
"sir" and "mister."
And so, instead, I gave my wish...

...To my little sister.

About the Author:
Adrianna Ahern Donat is a freelance writer. She is the mother of two boys who dreamed of what they'd do once they could grow facial hair. Adrianna has a husband, a dog, and a cat, all of whom are bewhiskered. Unlike William, she has not been able to experience the magic of her own facial hair (yet). She is the author of Medicine for Monster and is working on a young adult novel, neither of which have to do with hair.

About the Illustrator:
William Roth currently has a bushy beard, but he is not six. He is 18, going to art school, and plans to study illustration. He has been drawing since he was 3. When he was 12, he was commissioned to illustrate the 167page book How to Ruin a Business Without Really Trying, and also had his first solo art show. He knows Adrianna's son, and has given him hand-drawn birthday cards, which led Adrianna to think of him to illustrate this book.

Made in the USA
Middletown, DE
10 September 2019